To Katie

First U.S. edition 2003

Library of Congress Cataloging-in-Publication Data

Voake, Charlotte.
Ginger finds a home / Charlotte Voake. — 1st U.S. ed.
p.   cm.
Summary: A little girl feeds Ginger, a thin little cat who has been
living in a patch of weeds, and takes him home to live with her.
ISBN 0-7636-1999-X
[1. Cats — Fiction. 2. Pets — Fiction. 3. Animal rescue — Fiction.] I. Title.
PZ7.V855 Gk 2003
[E] — dc21   2002073898

2 4 6 8 10 9 7 5 3 1

Printed in China

This book was typeset in Calligraph810.
The illustrations were done in watercolor and ink.

Candlewick Press
2067 Massachusetts Avenue
Cambridge, Massachusetts 02140

visit us at www.candlewick.com

GINGER
finds a home

Charlotte Voake

CANDLEWICK PRESS
CAMBRIDGE, MASSACHUSETTS

Once there was
a little orange cat
who lived in
a patch of weeds
at the end
of a garden.

His ears were black
with dirt. He was very thin.
His fur stuck out.

His tail was like
a piece of
STRING!

He drank water
from puddles.
He looked in trash cans
for things to eat.

Every day he searched
for food,
and every night
he went back
to his patch of weeds
to sleep.

Then one day
everything
changed.

The little cat had found
only a bit of bread to eat,
and he was cold
and hungry as he came
back to his patch
of weeds.

He stopped.
There on the
ground was . . .

a plate of
delicious
cat food.

He couldn't believe his eyes!

He gobbled it up
and went to sleep.
He had never
slept so well!

The next night,
he found another
plate of food
waiting
for him . . .

and SOMETHING
ELSE.

A little
girl!

"Hello,"
she said.

She tried to stroke his fur,
but he was
frightened
and ran
to hide
in the
weeds.

"See you tomorrow,"
said the little girl.

She came to visit
him every day.
She brought him
nice things
to eat.

She
called him
Ginger.

Soon Ginger looked
forward to seeing
the little girl.
He came when
she called, and when
she stroked him,
he purred.

The little girl loved Ginger.

"Ginger," she said, "you can't stay here. Why don't you come home with me."

So Ginger followed
the little girl
home.

He had never
been in a house before.

He looked
in all the
corners and
under all
the furniture.
But poor
Ginger
was
so nervous . . .

that when the little girl
tried to shut
the door,

he ran out into
the garden as fast as he could.

The little girl looked outside. She couldn't see him anywhere. "Ginger!" she called.

But Ginger didn't come.

"I've frightened him away," she said. "He doesn't want to live with me."

The little girl
        was very sad.
        She was so upset
                she didn't notice . . .

when Ginger
   came creeping back in.

"Meow!"

said Ginger.

"GINGER!"

said the little girl.

Now Ginger
lives with
the little
girl in her
house.

He is a very
happy cat.

And the only time
  he ever goes back
  to the patch of weeds
    at the end
      of the garden . . .

is to

sunbathe!